# Goddess Girls

*The Goddess Girls Series*

Athena the Brain

Persephone the Phony

Aphrodite the Beauty

Artemis the Brave

# Goddess Girls

## APHRODITE
## THE BEAUTY

### JOAN HOLUB &
### SUZANNE WILLIAMS

www.atombooks.net/tween

ATOM

First published in the United States in 2010
First published in Great Britain in 2012 by Atom

A CIP catalogue record for this book
is available from the British Library.

ISBN 978-1-907411-48-9

Typeset in Baskerville Book by M Rules
Printed and bound in Great Britain by
Clays Ltd, St Ives plc

Papers used by Atom are from well-managed forests
and other responsible sources.

MIX
Paper from
responsible sources
FSC® C104740

Atom
An imprint of
Little, Brown Book Group
100 Victoria Embankment
London EC4Y 0DY

An Hachette UK Company
www.hachette.co.uk

www.atombooks.net/tween

To Emily Lawrence, editorial goddess

J. H. and S. W.

# CONTENTS

| | | |
|---|---|---|
| 1 | Boy Trouble | 1 |
| 2 | The Makeover | 17 |
| 3 | Party Time | 32 |
| 4 | Hippomenes | 48 |
| 5 | Gone Shopping | 62 |
| 6 | Gossip | 81 |
| 7 | The Olive Grove | 96 |
| 8 | An Argument | 110 |
| 9 | The Race | 121 |
| 10 | Perfect Matches | 134 |
| 11 | Red Roses | 143 |

# 1

## Boy Trouble

Aphrodite slid into her seat in Mr Cyclops's Hero-ology lesson just as the lyrebell sounded, signalling the start of another day at Mount Olympus Academy. As she tucked her long golden hair, which was threaded with pink ribbons, behind her delicate ears, she was aware that every godboy in the class was watching her. She hoped that in her rush to get ready that morning she hadn't got lipstick on her teeth. Lifting her chin, she smiled at one of the godboys. Because he was a centaur, and therefore part horse, he stood at the back of the room. With four legs, it was too difficult to sit in a chair. Dazzled by Aphrodite's attention and sparkling blue eyes, he blushed and glanced away.

A few of the bolder godboys continued to gaze at her, however. Their adoration was plain to see. Ignoring them, Aphrodite reached into her bag and took out her Hero-ology textscroll. As the goddessgirl of love and beauty, she'd grown used to such admiration. Took it for granted in fact. All her life, godboys had found her enchantingly beautiful. It seemed they had only to look at her to fall hopelessly in love. That wasn't her fault, of course. It was just the way things were.

Aphrodite glanced across the aisle at Athena, trying to get her attention. All week, the class discussions had centred around mortal maidens and youths. She wanted to ask if Athena had heard the intriguing rumours about a maiden on Earth who could run as swiftly as the wind, faster than any youth – or even beast. But as usual, her friend's nose was buried in a textscroll. Before Aphrodite could call out to her, Medusa, who sat directly behind Athena, leaned across the aisle.

Her head writhed with hissing green snakes instead of hair. Their tongues flicked in and out as she poked Aphrodite with one of her long green fingernails. "You were almost late," she sneered. "Troubles, Bubbles?" Medusa and her horrible sisters, Stheno and Euryale, never missed an opportunity to use the awful nickname to make fun of Aphrodite's sea-foam origins.

"Not really," Aphrodite muttered. She wasn't about to admit she'd overslept. It would only give Medusa another reason to poke fun at her. Probably with jokes about her needing lots of beauty sleep. Fortunately, before her snaky green nemesis could say anything more, Mr Cyclops finished with a student he'd been speaking to and stood up. As his humongous single eye swept the room, everyone fell silent.

Aphrodite wondered what they'd be discussing today. Yesterday their teacher had asked how much and what kind of help they thought gods should give to mortals they favoured. Aphrodite, who enjoyed helping mortals in love, had hoped to talk about that, but the godboys in the class had immediately steered the discussion towards weapons and war – topics that could never hold her interest for long.

Reaching into her bag again, she pulled out her pink papyrus notepad and began to doodle little hearts all over the front with her favourite red feather pen. Mr Cyclops cleared his throat. "Today I'd like you to consider the following question," he said. "Need mortal maidens always marry?"

Dropping her red feather pen in surprise, Aphrodite sat up straighter. Now this was an engaging question! She'd like to see the godboys try to make *this* into a discussion about weapons and war, she thought, as she raised her hand high.

"Yes, Aphrodite?" asked Mr Cyclops.

"I wouldn't want to see any young maiden go unwed," she said. "Everyone should have a chance to fall in love."

"But what if the maiden would rather be alone?" Athena asked. "What if she has other interests, like

5

travelling the world, or becoming a first-class scholar, or ... or inventing things?"

Aphrodite smiled at her. Poor Athena. She'd never really had a boyfriend. Just wait until she experienced her first crush. She'd think differently then. "If the maiden feels that way, then perhaps it's only because she hasn't yet found the right youth," Aphrodite said kindly.

"But not all youths marry," Athena pointed out. "So why should all maidens?"

Poseidon thrust his trident into the air. As always, water dripped from it and him to puddle beneath his chair. "That's because many youths prefer the life of a soldier," he declared.

"That's right!" exclaimed another godboy. "War trumps marriage any day."

Aphrodite rolled her eyes. "Oh, really? And

which do you think contributes more to the survival of the human race?"

Mr Cyclops beamed at her. "Good point."

Just then the school intercom crackled to life. "Attention, godboys and goddessgirls!" thundered Principal Zeus in a deafeningly loud voice. Everyone, including Mr Cyclops, automatically reached up to cover their ears. "A special assembly on chariot safety starts in ten minutes. Please make your way to the auditorium."

Looking somewhat annoyed, Mr Cyclops muttered something about unwarranted interruptions to class time. But then, with a sigh, he said, "All right, everyone. Please line up at the door."

Normally, Aphrodite would have welcomed a chance to get out of a lesson, but not today. Not when the topic of discussion was such an interesting one. Besides, the chariot safety assembly was repeated every year, and it was deadly dull. Who among them didn't know that racing into a turn could cause a chariot to tip over? Duh. Or that you shouldn't ever fly directly into the sun?

After the assembly, which Zeus had livened up with a real demonstration of racing chariots for a change, it was time for lunch. Aphrodite was starving. As she stood in the cafeteria queue with Athena and their other two best friends, dark-haired Artemis and pale-skinned Persephone, her stomach began to rumble like a volcano about to erupt.

Her friends laughed. "*Somebody's* hungry," said Artemis.

Aphrodite blushed. "Yes, very." She didn't say it loudly, but considering the response, she might just as well have shouted it. A dozen godboys in the queue ahead of her whipped around at the sound of her voice, eager to get her attention.

"You can have my spot, Aphrodite!" yelled Poseidon from ten spaces in front.

He took a step towards her, dripping water on to another godboy's sandal-clad feet. Ares, who was the cutest godboy in school in Aphrodite's opinion, glowered at him. "Watch where you're dripping, Fishface!" Droplets of water flew as he shook one foot and then the other. Poseidon glowered back, his mouth opening and closing like a fish's.

Ignoring him, Ares turned towards Aphrodite. "Take my place," he said with a charming smile. "I insist."

Aphrodite hesitated. Ares could be a bit of a bully at times, but she had to admit there was something about him she found . . . well, *irresistible*. He was just so muscular, so blond, and so blue eyed. Smiling uncertainly, she took a step in his direction.

Athena grabbed Aphrodite's elbow. "Surely you're not going to take him up on that," she said in a low voice that Ares couldn't hear. "It wouldn't be fair to the other goddessgirls ahead of us."

"Oh. I guess you're right," said Aphrodite. She'd just stepped back into the queue when a godboy named Atlas called out, "Hey, Aphrodite! Come and stand with me!" Flexing his bulging biceps, he picked up the scrawny godboy next to him and held him over his head. "You can have Hephaestus's place."

Squirming this way and that, Hephaestus protested, "Put me down, you big ox."

Aphrodite sighed. "For the love of Zeus! Leave him alone, Atlas."

Atlas shrugged. "If you say so." He set Hephaestus down, but not before a fight broke out between Poseidon and Ares.

"Godness!" exclaimed Persephone, anxiously twisting a red curl around her index finger. "Someone's going to get hurt!"

Frowning, Aphrodite took a step towards the boys. "Persephone's right. Stop it! Where do you think you are – at nursery school?"

Sheepishly, the two godboys separated. In a voice as lovely as she was, but which permitted no argument, she said, "I appreciate the offers, but I'll wait my turn like everyone else."

Ten minutes later, when she was seated at last with her three goddessgirl friends at their favourite table in the cafeteria, Aphrodite dipped her spoon into the delicious yambrosia. After

11

she'd taken only a bite or two, however, she shoved the bowl away, too annoyed to finish in spite of her hunger.

"Full already?" asked Artemis, as she dug with gusto into her own bowl. Her three dogs, a bloodhound, a greyhound and a beagle, lay at her feet. They accompanied her everywhere.

"No, just fed up with godboys," Aphrodite declared. "They're so obsessed with weapons and war. They even battle for my attention!"

"Poor you," Persephone teased between sips of nectar. "A lot of goddessgirls would die to have godboys notice them." As an afterthought, she added, "But of course they can't, since they're all immortal."

Athena set down the shimmery blue Beauty-ology textscroll she'd been scanning as she ate. With a puzzled look she said to Aphrodite, "But I thought you liked the attention."

Aphrodite shrugged. "Not really. If another godboy offers to carry my scrolls or to help me with my homework just one more time today, I swear I'll scream!"

"Really?" Athena leaned forward, her brows knitted. "But in Hero-ology class you said that everyone should have the chance to fall in love."

"I was talking about mortals," said Aphrodite. "And anyway, just because a godboy fusses over you, it doesn't mean he's in love with you." Indeed, she couldn't help wondering if the handsome young godboys who fluttered around her like moths to a flame might disappear in a flash if she weren't beautiful. There was no way to know because she'd always been ... well ... naturally pretty.

"But most girls like it when boys fuss over them," Athena persisted. She seemed oddly interested in the topic given her protest that "some maidens" would rather be left alone to study.

Aphrodite raised one of her perfectly shaped eyebrows. "If I didn't know any better, I'd think maybe *you* wanted to be fussed over."

"Who, me? Ha!" said Athena. "That's the last thing on my mind," she murmured as she buried her nose in her Beauty-ology scroll again.

Aphrodite swapped amused glances with Persephone and Artemis, who then quickly moved on to talk about other things. But Aphrodite only half listened as she stared at Athena's bent head. A straight-A student, Athena was easily the brightest of the four friends. She was also the youngest, though they were all in the same year. Until this moment,

Athena had never shown any curiosity about godboys, and they in turn, probably sensing her indifference, overlooked her.

Athena glanced up from her textscroll. "What?" she asked. "Why are you staring at me like that?"

"No reason," Aphrodite said lightly. But as Athena returned to her textscroll, the wheels in Aphrodite's brain began to spin faster than the racing chariot Zeus had driven in assembly that morning. Within moments she concluded that Athena had in fact been hinting that she'd welcome the attention of godboys. And while Aphrodite might be fed up with godboys' annoying antics, she loved stirring up romance for others! True, things hadn't worked out so well between Paris and Helen – that pesky Trojan War and all – but at least she'd *tried* to set them up.

*That's it*! she thought excitedly. If she could help

*mortals* find love, then why not a goddessgirl, too? She could use her talents to help Athena find her first crush! But she would need a game plan.

Aphrodite drummed her well-manicured, powder-pink-polished fingernails on the tabletop, sneaking glances at Athena's long, unstyled brown hair. At her face free of make-up. At her frumpy, plain white chiton. Suddenly an idea came to her. A makeover! That was exactly what her friend needed to make MOA's godboys sit up and take notice.

Now that she'd come up with a plan, Aphrodite couldn't wait to get started!

# 2

# The Makeover

When school finished, Aphrodite and her friends walked up the marble staircase to the goddessgirls' dorm on the fourth floor. Halfway up, Aphrodite announced, "I think we should give Athena a makeover."

"A w-what?" asked Athena, almost dropping the bag of scrolls she was carrying.

"A makeover," Aphrodite repeated. "Hair, nails, make-up, clothes – the works! What do you say? We'll create a whole new you!"

"What a great idea!" said Persephone, patting her own reddish curls.

"Better her than me," said Artemis, adjusting the quiver of arrows and archery bow she always carried over one shoulder. Her three hounds leaped up the stairs at her heels, drooly tongues hanging out. Aphrodite kept as far away from them as possible.

Athena frowned. "What's wrong with the old me?"

"Nothing," Aphrodite said quickly, "but don't you think it would be fun to try a new look?"

Athena hesitated, shifting her load of scrolls from one arm to the other. Glancing down at her Beauty-ology scroll, she rubbed her thumb over its blue ribbon. "Well, maybe," she said at last. "I mean I *would* like to learn more about the ins and outs of beauty."

"Great. What better time than now?" asked Aphrodite.

When they reached her door, Artemis said, "I'll leave the dogs in my room. Unless of course ... " She glanced at Aphrodite.

"Good idea," Aphrodite said quickly, guessing Artemis was about to ask if her dogs could watch the makeover too. Most students shared a room, and she and Artemis were supposed to have been roommates, but Aphrodite hadn't wanted to share space with three smelly, messy dogs. So Artemis had taken the free room next door.

After Artemis dropped off her dogs, the four

goddessgirls went into Aphrodite's room. All the dorm rooms on the fourth and fifth floors were identical, with two beds, two wardrobes and two built-in desks. To decorate, Aphrodite had draped sparkly red fabric over her bed and painted pink and red hearts all over the walls.

"I don't know how you keep your room so neat," Artemis told her. "Mine's always a mess."

"We know," teased Aphrodite. "We've seen it." Unlike most other goddessgirls, Aphrodite always put her belongings away and swept her floor and dusted once a week. She even made her bed each morning, arranging the six puffy, heart-shaped pillows on it just so. In truth, she was a bit of a perfectionist when it came to her room and her looks.

"Must be nice to live in a dorm," Persephone

commented. She lived at home with her mother, Demeter. Flopping on to one of Aphrodite's beds, she sank into the plush red velvet blanket stitched with a pattern of little white hearts. "Mmm, comfy," she said.

Aphrodite handed Persephone and Artemis a few issues of *Teen Scrollazine* from the shelf above her desk. "See if you can find any hairstyles that you think would look good on Athena."

"Aye-aye, Captain Makeover," Artemis said with a grin. She sat beside Persephone, and they began flipping through the pages, discussing the pros and cons of various hairstyles.

Aphrodite went to her spare desk, which she'd converted to a make-up table years ago. Neatly arranged on a silver tray atop a length of tasselled pink satin were rows and rows of nail polish and lipsticks in every conceivable colour, and dozens of little pots of eyeshadow, blusher and moisturiser.

"You can sit here," she told Athena, pulling out the stool from the desk and patting its seat.

Athena sank on to the cushioned stool and stared at all the cosmetics. "Ye gods! You've got enough stuff to open your own make-up shop." She picked up a round, silver box that sat to one side of the tray. "What's in here?"

As soon as she spoke the words, the box's lid popped off and a silver-handled make-up brush flew out. Hovering a few centimetres above the pots of blusher, it regarded Athena critically. Then, seeming to make a decision, it dipped into an orangey-pink one and swirled around. Then it zoomed closer to whisk its powder high along Athena's cheekbone.

"Hey, stop!" she cried, raising both hands and ducking away.

The make-up brush froze in mid-air, its bristles bent in the shape of a question mark.

Aphrodite laughed. "We're not quite ready yet," she told it. "After we do her hair."

With a quick nod, the brush ducked back into its box and the lid snapped shut.

Aphrodite fingered a lock of Athena's long brown hair and frowned. "You should take better care of it," she said. "It's dry."

"Really?" Athena combed her fingers through her hair, testing it herself. "I never noticed."

"That's because your nose is always stuck in a textscroll," said Aphrodite. "Do you ever even look in a mirror?"

"Not very often," Athena admitted. Cocking her

head, she asked, "How often would you say *you* look into one?"

"Me?" Aphrodite asked, realising with a start that she'd been checking her lustrous waves in the mirror above her make-up table at that very moment. It was like an automatic reflex! She looked away from her reflection, a little embarrassed. "I don't know."

Aphrodite sprayed some conditioner into Athena's hair. "*Mmm*, that smells good," said Athena. "What is it?"

"Essence of Hyacinth," Aphrodite replied, combing it through. "It's the best conditioner I've found. Not only does it smell good, but it also leaves your hair really soft and manageable."

"Essence of Hyacinth," Athena repeated. "Could you write that down for me?"

Delighted at her interest, Aphrodite took a sheet

of sparkly pink papyrus from a drawer in her desk and jotted down the name of the conditioner with her red feather pen. "Here," she said, handing the papyrus and her pen to Athena. "In case you want to make more notes as we go along."

"Thanks," said Athena, setting them on her lap. "I just might."

"We've chosen six possible hairstyles," Persephone announced, bringing over several of the scrollazines.

After a quick look at them, Athena pointed to a painting of a goddess with her hair pinned high on top of her head. "I think I'd like to try this style."

"Okay." Aphrodite grabbed her Spell-ology textscroll from the top of her desk and unfurled it. "Use this one," she said, pointing to a spell. Then she handed her friend a silver-backed hand mirror.

Looking into the mirror, Athena read the chant aloud: "Magic mirror, let me see ... how this style would look on me."

As Athena's words died away, Aphrodite touched the painting to the centre of the mirror. When she lifted it again, she said, "Take a look."

Athena peered at her reflection. Laughing, she reached up to touch her magically restyled hair. "No good. I look like someone's mother."

"You're right," agreed Persephone. "In fact, you could be *my* mother."

"Looks like you're wearing a beehive on your head," added Artemis.

"Ye gods!" said Athena, giggling.

"Let's see the others," suggested Aphrodite. After trying a few more hairstyles, they finally found the perfect one.

"Fabulous!" said Aphrodite. "I like how the layers frame your face."

"Yes," said Persephone. "And long fringes are so glamorous."

"You look like a different person," said Artemis. "In a good way."

Athena smiled at herself in the mirror. "Thanks." She smoothed a hand over her feathery new hairdo. Then she reached for the pink papyrus and Aphrodite's pen, quickly making notes. "What's next?" she asked, obviously getting into the spirit of things.

As if it had been waiting for these very words, the make-up brush sprang out of its box again. It went to work, dusting Athena's cheeks with a medium shade of blusher, then brushing her eyelids with a sparkly grey eyeshadow that was slightly darker than her eyes. As Athena scribbled more notes, Persephone gave her a thumbs up. "Looking great!"

Glancing at the brush, Aphrodite nodded her approval as well. "Good job." Its bristles curved into a smile before it hopped back into its box.

Next Persephone began to work on Athena's nails, filing and painting them. In the meantime, Aphrodite flung open both of her wardrobes and pulled out one chiton after another for Athena to try on. Artemis, however, seemed to have lost interest in the makeover. After poking through all the stuff on top of Aphrodite's make-up table, she grabbed a small glazed pot and retired with it to the spare bed.

When her nails were dry, Athena stepped behind a folding screen painted with delicate pink rosebuds to try on the various outfits Aphrodite had selected for her. "How about this one?" she asked, modelling a chiton the colour of daffodils.

Aphrodite shook her head. "Yellow's good on Persephone, but it doesn't suit you. Where's that turquoise one?" she mumbled, searching through her wardrobes again.

"Probably in your remote wardrobe," said Artemis. She was sitting cross-legged on Aphrodite's spare bed, waxing the string of her bow.

"That better not be my leg wax," said Aphrodite, pulling her head out of the wardrobe.

"Oops, sorry," Artemis said meekly. She set aside the little pot she'd taken from the desk earlier.

"Remote wardrobe?" Persephone belatedly echoed.

"I let Aphrodite use my extra wardrobe for her overflow as I don't need it," Artemis explained. With that, she dashed off to her room, reappearing moments later with the turquoise chiton.

Athena's eyes lit up when she saw it. She tried it on behind the screen and came out twirling.

"Perfect," said Aphrodite. "Turquoise looks great on you!" Digging through a drawer, she found some silver combs for Athena's hair and also a silver belt with hammered links in the shape of leaves.

"You look fantastic!" Persephone said when Athena's makeover was complete.

Busily filing an arrow tip with one of Aphrodite's nail files, Artemis barely glanced up, but even she seemed impressed by the transformation. "Yeah, you do look nice, Athena."

Gazing into the large mirror above the make-up table, Athena turned this way and that, studying her reflection. "Wow," she said. "I look ... *sophisticated*."

The others laughed. "Just wait till everyone else sees you!" said Aphrodite.

Persephone snapped her fingers. "That reminds me. Today's Friday, right? Hades told me there's a party tonight in the godboys' dorm on the fifth floor. We could go and show off Athena."

"Great idea!" Aphrodite exclaimed. "How about it, Athena?"

Athena hesitated, as if a little unsure. "I suppose so."

"All right!" said Aphrodite. She could hardly wait for everyone to admire the work she'd done on her friend. A godboy or two was certain to notice the transformation. With any luck, this could turn out to be the night of Athena's first crush. And it would all be thanks to Aphrodite!

# 3

## Party Time

When the goddessgirls met up after dinner, Athena's roommate, Pandora (one of the few mortals at MOA), came too. "How did you make Athena look so fabulous?" she asked Aphrodite as the girls climbed the stairs to the fifth floor. Before Aphrodite could reply, Pandora plowed ahead, "This party should be a lot of fun, don't you think? Won't it be great if there's a band playing? Hey, could you do my hair and make-up sometime?"

"Uh, of course," said Aphrodite. Her reply would've worked for *any* of the questions. With Pandora it didn't really matter anyway. She was always so busy asking questions that she never paid much attention to the answers she received. As if a sign of her curiosity, her fringe, streaked blue and gold like the rest of her hair, was plastered against her forehead in the shape of a question mark.

The party was in the common area at the end of the boys' hallway. Loud voices and laughter greeted their ears as the goddessgirls approached. But as Aphrodite led her friends into the room, a hushed silence fell over the godboys and goddessgirls milling around the snack table and perched on sofas. Aphrodite was used to causing a stir wherever she

33

went – especially if godboys were present – but this time everyone seemed to be looking at Athena.

Staring at Athena in open-mouthed surprise, Poseidon did a double take and dropped his trident. It clattered to the floor, barely missing the lizard-like tail of another godboy, who flicked his forked tongue in annoyance at him and then scuttled away. "Wow, Athena," Poseidon said at last. "You look really ... different!"

"Is that a compliment or an insult?" Athena teased, but Aphrodite noticed she was blushing.

"A compliment," Poseidon said quickly. "Let me get you some nectar and some crisps," he said as several other godboys gathered around to fawn over Athena.

"How about some grapes?" offered Dionysus, a godboy with curly black hair and small horns.

"Want to sit by me?" asked Atlas.

Lifting one of the sofas, he tipped it forward so that the godboy and goddessgirl who had been sitting on it together slid off. "Hey!" they cried as they landed on the floor.

Ignoring them, Atlas lowered the sofa. "See, plenty of space."

Aphrodite couldn't help grinning in delight. It seemed she'd succeeded in making Athena irresistible. And she wasn't even wearing any of Aphrodite's Lucky-in-Love lip gloss!

Unused to the increased attention, Athena seemed a bit flustered. When Artemis's twin brother, Apollo, offered her a seat next to him, she replied, "No thanks. I prefer to stand."

*Poor girl*, thought Aphrodite. Athena could really do with some pointers on how to flirt! She glanced around the room. There were only a few godboys who seemed oblivious to Athena's charms. One of them was Hades. Dark and brooding, he'd had a crush on Persephone for weeks now. The two of them were huddled together near the punch bowl, deep in conversation. Kneeling nearby, Artemis was feeding crisps to her dogs.

"Hey, everybody!"

Aphrodite's eyes sparkled as Ares entered the room. He really was the cutest godboy in all of MOA. A beefy godboy named Kydoimos and a squinty-eyed one named Makhai followed in his wake. "Hi, Ares!" she called out, waving to him.

To her embarrassment, he didn't seem to notice her. His gorgeous blue eyes settled on Athena and stayed there. "Well, well!" he said, speaking loud enough for everyone to hear. "Who's the new girl?"

Kydoimos and Makhai laughed. But Aphrodite wasn't so sure Ares was joking. He'd never paid any attention to Athena before. It wouldn't surprise her if he really didn't recognise her. As she watched him saunter over to Athena, Aphrodite got a tight feeling in her chest. Surely she couldn't be . . . *jealous* of one of her best friends? Over a godboy?

"Um, hello, Aphrodite," someone said from beside her.

She turned to look. It was Hephaestus, the skinny godboy Atlas had hefted over his head in the lunch queue as if he weighed less than a feather pillow. Which, from the look of him, he probably did. "Oh, hi," said Aphrodite. Hearing the disappointment in her own voice, she smiled, hoping to cover it up. "Nice party, huh?" she said brightly. But her eyes kept flicking back to

Ares and Athena. What were they saying to each other?

Hephaestus nodded. "Especially now that you're here," he said. Then he blushed.

"Uh-huh, thanks," said Aphrodite. Normally, scrawny little godboys like Hephaestus didn't speak to her. It was as if they guessed – rightly, she had to admit – that they didn't stand a chance with her. Not when all she had to do to make even the handsomest of godboys fall for her was look in his direction and smile. Did that make her shallow? she wondered. Once Artemis had accused her of being overly concerned with outward appearances. Uncomfortably, she remembered Athena's question about how often she looked at herself in a mirror. Still, why shouldn't she choose the handsomest boys when she could pick whomever she liked?

"Want something to eat?" Hephaestus asked. "Some crisps and ambrosia dip?"

"Sure, why not," said Aphrodite. She studied him curiously as he moved towards the table, limping slightly. He was lame in both legs. If she were being honest, he was also not very good-looking. His forehead was too high, his chin too weak, and his eyes too close together. Still, none of the other godboys were paying any attention to her right now. Tonight their eyes were only for Athena.

"Ha!" Ares's voice boomed out. "Good one, Theeny!" *Theeny?* Principal Zeus was the only one who called Athena that. And *he* was her father. What did it mean that Ares was using the nickname? Glancing towards the sofa where Athena now sat surrounded by half a dozen godboys, Aphrodite watched Ares lean in and rest his hand on

Athena's shoulder. Aphrodite gritted her teeth. Athena could have any godboy she wanted, but *not* Ares.

As Athena smiled up at him, Aphrodite's stomach somersaulted. Suddenly, she couldn't stand being at the party a moment longer. She headed for the door, completely forgetting Hephaestus and not noticing that she'd left him standing in the middle of the room, balancing two plates of snacks.

When Pandora saw her leaving, she leaped up from her chair. "Hey, where are you going? Don't you like the party? Aren't you having fun?"

Everyone heard her, of course. They all stopped talking and looked in Aphrodite's direction. "I'm just a little tired, okay?" said Aphrodite, trying to shush her. "I'm going to my room."

Persephone and Artemis stared at her in surprise,

40

but Athena called out, "Wait up. I'll go with you!" She rose from the sofa, but immediately a throng of godboys began begging her to stay.

"Please don't go," said Poseidon. "You haven't told us about your newest inventions yet."

"And I want to hear more about that town the Greek mortals named after you," Ares said, his voice oozing with admiration.

"Athens? Oh, all right, I guess I can stay a few more minutes." Sounding only a little reluctant, she settled on to the sofa again.

Aphrodite hesitated, waiting for the godboys – especially one *particular* godboy with blond hair and blue eyes – to beg her to stay too. But none of them did. Feeling humiliated, she rushed the rest of the way to the open door. Unfortunately, Medusa chose just that moment to arrive with Stheno and Euryale.

41

The triplets all had skin the colour of spring leaves, but only Medusa had snakes for hair. Rattling and hissing, they coiled and uncoiled around her head, forming different hairstyles at whim.

With a little yelp, Pandora ducked her head and ran to the back of the room. The snakes gave Medusa the power to turn mortals to stone if they happened to look into her eyes. Because they were mortal, Artemis's dogs were susceptible too. "Drop and cover, boys," Artemis commanded. Immediately, all three hounds lay down on the floor and covered their eyes with their paws.

Still standing in the doorway, the triplets blocked Aphrodite's escape. "Leaving already, Bubbles?" Medusa asked with a smirk. One of her snakes lunged towards Aphrodite, flicking its tongue at her.

Eyeing it warily, though it could do her no harm,

Aphrodite gritted her teeth. "That's right. Please move so I can get past."

Medusa swept her gaze over the crowd, obviously relishing an audience. "Certainly. Far be it from me to add to your troubles, Bubbles." Stheno and Euryale cackled as if she'd just cracked the funniest joke ever.

"Know something?" Aphrodite retorted, thinking about the time, several weeks ago, when Medusa had got her just desserts, "I think I liked you better as a statue!" Squeezing past the triplets, she fled the room. Tears brimmed in her eyes. She'd wanted godboys to notice Athena, but she hadn't thought it would mean they'd ignore *her*! Especially Ares. This wasn't at all what she'd imagined happening when she decided to help Athena out. How could things have gone so wrong?

When she reached her room, Aphrodite collapsed on to her bed. But before she could give vent to her tears, her window began to rattle violently. Startled, she rolled off the bed and leaped to her feet. Suddenly, the window blew open and a strange, glittery breeze whooshed in, bringing with it a rolled-up piece of papyrus. "Art thou Aphrodite, goddessgirl of love?" the wind howled.

Too stunned to reply, Aphrodite merely nodded. Abruptly, the breeze stilled. "The mortal Hippomenes petitions thee for help," it said. Then it dropped the papyrus and whooshed back out of the window as fast as it had entered.

Aphrodite caught the scroll as it floated towards the floor. Unrolling it quickly, she began to read:

Dear Aphrodite, Immortal Goddess and
Champion of Lovers,

Please hear my plea. I am in love with a
beautiful mortal maiden named Atalanta. I wish
to marry her, but she has vowed to take as
husband only the youth who beats her in a
race, and she is very fleet of foot.

Her father, King Schoeneus, has made a law
that those who lose against her shall also lose
their lives. I am prepared to forfeit my life for
love but would really rather not. So, I'm hoping
for your divine assistance in this matter.

Your devoted follower,
Hippomenes

Aphrodite sighed. *How romantic.* Ares could certainly learn a few lessons from this mortal! Suddenly it struck her that this Atalanta was likely the maiden of the rumours – the one who ran as swiftly as the wind. Interesting! Grabbing her bag, she fished around in it for her red feather pen. Then she dashed off a reply on a sheet of pink papyrus:

Dear Hippomenes,

Your appeal has gone straight to my heart.
I will meet you at the racecourse behind
King Schoeneus's palace tomorrow morning
at eight to discuss your request.

Immortally yours,
Aphrodite

After rereading her note, she worried that her tone was too informal and not commanding enough. Mortals always seemed to expect gods and goddesses to issue orders. Well, she could fix that. She added a postscript:

P.S. Don't be late!

*That should do it*, she thought. She rolled up the sheet of papyrus, tied it with a red ribbon, and then stepped to the open window with it. Holding it loosely, she chanted the Send spell: "*Blow wind, blow. Off you go. Deliver this message, and don't be slow.*"

Immediately a breeze whisked the papyrus scroll from her outstretched hand and carried it away.

# 4

# Hippomenes

Aphrodite woke early the next morning. Remembering her promise to meet Hippomenes, she climbed out of bed and dressed quickly with barely a glance at the mirror above her make-up table. Artemis's dogs were whining next door. Usually Artemis was up at the crack of dawn to take them for their morning walk, but she'd probably come home late from the party and was still asleep. Maybe she could quieten them before they woke anyone else, thought Aphrodite.

Going next door, she knocked lightly and then opened Artemis's door a crack. Before she could stop them, the boisterous dogs pushed it wider and rushed into the hall, yapping and bouncing around in high spirits. Lying tangled in her bedcovers, Artemis just snuffled and rolled over in her sleep.

"Shh!" Aphrodite tried to gather the three hounds, but it was impossible to catch them. Seeming to think it was all a game, they tore off through the hall and down four flights of stairs. "Stop!" she called, keeping her voice low so as not to wake the entire dorm as she chased after them.

The dogs completely ignored her. When she finally caught up with them by the main hall entrance, she couldn't get them to go back upstairs, no matter how much she tugged at their collars. And from the way they were scratching at the door and whining, it was obvious they had to go to the bathroom.

"Okay, okay," she said. "But just for a minute. Then you have to come right back in. Promise?" If they were quick about their business, she'd still have plenty of time to meet Hippomenes at eight.

The hounds wagged their tails as if in agreement. However, the second she opened the academy's bronze doors, all three of them dashed outside in different directions.

"Come back! Bad dogs!" Tails between their legs, the greyhound and the beagle paused at the bottom of the granite steps to wait for her, but Suez, the bloodhound, was in particularly high spirits and took off across the courtyard. Aphrodite had no choice but to chase after him. The other two dogs followed, stopping here and there to sniff things along the way.

A trail lined with trees and bushes started at the far side of the courtyard and wound down Mount Olympus. Aphrodite glimpsed Suez's backside as he vanished down the trail. The rascal's tail was wagging – probably proud of himself for making such a grand escape!

"If I'm late meeting Hippomenes it will be all your fault!" she called after him. But her words had no effect. Eventually, she caught up with him when he stopped by a bush to lift his leg. Folding her arms, she scolded him. "So you just had to come all the way out here to this particular bush to do your business, huh? You couldn't possibly use one of the bushes right by the school?"

She had planned to take the dogs back inside before meeting up with Hippomenes, but she was already halfway to Earth. If she went back to the dorm now, she'd be late for sure. "All right," she said, "I guess you'll be coming with me." She hoped Artemis wouldn't wake before they returned and wonder where her hounds had got to. The dogs wagged their tails, obviously happy to prolong their adventure. Even Suez seemed content to trot along beside her now as they continued down the trail.

It was just past eight when they reached King Schoeneus's palace. At the edge of the sandy racecourse on the far side of the palace a young man sat waiting. Aphrodite was pleased to see that

Hippomenes was on time. He was a handsome youth with chiselled features and light brown hair. Glancing at the dogs with a puzzled look, he leaped up to meet her. "You must be Artemis!" His eyes shone with wonder. "Forgive me for staring," he said. "I've never met a goddess before. And I was expecting Aphrodite!"

"That's me," said Aphrodite. "But the dogs do belong to Artemis. Down, Amby!" she said as the beagle stood up on his hind feet and pressed his forepaws against Hippomenes's knees. Amby liked attention almost as much as he did food.

"It's all right," said Hippomenes, laughing. He gently pushed Amby off, then knelt beside him. The dog immediately flopped down in the sand and rolled on to his back so that the youth could rub his belly. "It's wonderful of you to come," Hippomenes said to Aphrodite as he good-naturedly obliged the dog. "I can't thank you enough."

"You're welcome," she replied. She liked this young man's good manners and his easy laugh. She was inclined to grant his request for help right away, but there was something she needed to know first. "The young maiden you're in love with, this Atalanta," she said. "Does she return your love?"

Hippomenes ducked his head. "I ... I'm not sure," he said. "She pleaded with me not to enter the race. She said she was not worthy of the price."

"I see," said Aphrodite. She watched idly as Suez and Nectar, the greyhound, trotted over to a nearby stream and began to lap up water. Amby, however, was content to continue with his belly rub. It seemed to Aphrodite that Atalanta would not have said what she had unless she cared about what happened to Hippomenes.

Aphrodite fingered the double-*G* goddessgirl charm that hung from the delicate golden chain she wore around her neck. "And is she honest, your Atalanta?" she asked thoughtfully.

Hippomenes's eyes shone with love. "As honest as a mirror."

Actually, that was too bad, thought Aphrodite. If Atalanta was *that* honest she'd be unlikely to slow her pace to deliberately let Hippomenes win. "Are you fast enough to beat her?" she asked.

The youth hesitated. Amby looked up at him and licked his hand. Then the beagle stood and stretched. "I am fast," Hippomenes said, rising to his feet as Amby wandered off to join the other two hounds. "But Atalanta, I fear, is faster. Still, I will give it my all and die trying if I must."

Aphrodite shook her head. "That won't be necessary, I hope. When will the race take place?"

"Just after dawn in three days," said Hippomenes. "Does this mean you'll help me, O Gracious Goddess?"

With more confidence than she felt – after all, she had no plan as of yet – Aphrodite nodded. "I shall return before the start of the race."

Hippomenes fell to his knees. "Thank you, oh thank you."

*His gratitude and respect speak well of him*, thought Aphrodite as she turned to go. Such qualities would make him a good husband, as Atalanta must surely know. As Aphrodite passed beneath one of the palace windows a minute later, she heard someone sobbing piteously. Glancing up, she saw a beautiful young woman, with hair as long and golden as her own, gazing wistfully down at Hippomenes as he began to stretch his legs beside the track, preparing for a practice run.

The young woman must be Atalanta, of course. And her tears put to rest the question of her feelings towards Hippomenes. Leaving the palace grounds, Aphrodite began to jog back up the trail. Suez, Nectar and Amby trotted along behind her, their tongues hanging out. They were almost to the top of Mount Olympus when Hephaestus came limping towards them on a silver cane. Without thinking, Aphrodite said the first thing that popped into her head. "Out for a run?"

Immediately, she regretted her mistake. She clapped both hands over her mouth as if to recall the words. Hephaestus, however, only laughed and blithely waved his cane in the air. "Actually," he said, "I'm out for a *hobble*. Want to join me?"

Aphrodite hesitated. "I really should get the dogs back up to Artemis." He looked so disappointed that she quickly added, "But you could walk me to the dorm if you'd like."

Hephaestus's thin face lit up. "I'd love to." The dogs bounced on ahead of them as they headed back to the academy. Aphrodite walked slowly to make it easy for Hephaestus to keep up with her. He seemed a little tongue-tied, so to put him at ease, she began telling him about Hippomenes and his request for help. "The thing is," she said when she finished her story, "I want to help him, but I'm not really sure how to."

Hephaestus looked at her with shy admiration. "You'll think of something. You're very clever."

"Why, thanks," said Aphrodite, though she wasn't quite sure what she'd done to make him think so highly of her. Still, she couldn't help feeling pleased. She was used to compliments on her beauty, but no godboy had ever told her she was clever before.

"And if there's anything I can do to help you with this," Hephaestus continued, "you have only to ask."

"That's nice of you," said Aphrodite. "I'll keep your offer in mind." Truthfully, though, she doubted she'd have any reason to take him up on it.

Until this moment, her dealings with Hippomenes had pushed all thoughts of the party from her mind. But now they suddenly flooded back. She cringed to think how upset she'd been just because Ares had flirted with Athena. So what? She knew better than anyone that flirting didn't mean a thing. "Anything interesting happen after I left the party last night?" she heard herself ask.

Hephaestus looked down at his hands. "I don't know. I left not long after you did."

An awkward silence fell between them. To fill it, and to take her mind off her own problems, she said, "That's a beautiful cane." Etched into the silver in intricate detail, leaves and flowering vines wound the shaft from top to bottom.

"Thanks," he said. "Made it myself."

"I should've guessed," said Aphrodite, remembering that he was the god of blacksmiths and metalworking.

"I love forging things from metal," said Hephaestus. "It's so satisfying to transform a boring lump of gold or silver into something beautiful."

Aphrodite nodded. She could understand that feeling. After all, hadn't she got a lot of pleasure from transforming Athena last night? She and Hephaestus just worked with different *materials* – he with metals, she with make-up.

"Heading up?" she asked as they reached the granite steps leading to the academy's bronze doors.

He shook his head. "Later. I'm going to keep walking. It's good for my legs."

"Well, I'm glad I ran into you," she told him. And it was true. It was nice to talk to a godboy she didn't feel she had to flirt with, someone who thought she was *clever*. It made for a pleasant change.

"Me too." He smiled, waiting until she got inside before turning to continue his walk.

# 5

# Gone Shopping

It was past ten when Aphrodite got back upstairs, but Artemis was just waking up. Wagging their tails, the dogs leaped on to her bed and began licking her face. Hugging them, Artemis looked at Aphrodite in surprise. "You took them out?"

Aphrodite nodded. But before she could tell Artemis all that had happened that morning, her friend jumped out of bed. "You won't believe what happened last night after you left the party," she said, as she yanked open her wardrobe. A small heap of clean but wrinkled chitons lay at the bottom. She grabbed the first one she touched and slipped it on.

Aphrodite's muscles tensed. What if it was something concerning Ares and Athena? "What happened?" she asked, as Artemis's head popped out of the chiton's neckline.

Artemis grinned. "Poseidon and Dionysus decided to go swimming in one of the fountains. It was hilarious. I think they were showing off for Athena's benefit."

Feeling somewhat relieved, Aphrodite crossed to the open wardrobe and automatically began picking up the chitons. One by one, she shook out their wrinkles, then hung them up. "I bet she wasn't impressed."

"You got that right." Artemis poured water into a trough for her dogs, then scooped dry dog food into a large ceramic bowl. The hounds immediately ran over to slurp the water and gobble their food. As if to make up for his smaller size, Amby ate twice as fast as the other two. Artemis turned back towards Aphrodite. "She said it was obvious they'd missed getting brains the day they were handed out, probably because they were only being given to godboys who'd use them."

Aphrodite laughed. She resisted the urge to clean up the bits of soggy food that the dogs, especially Amby, were scattering around the bowl. "Did Ares go swimming with them?" she asked casually.

"Ares?" Artemis repeated absently as she reached

under her desk for her quiver of arrows. "No, for once he had more sense than the other godboys. Medusa got drenched though. She kept flirting with Poseidon, and I think he got tired of it. Anyway, he and Dionysus finally just picked her up and threw her in."

Aphrodite smiled. She would've liked to have seen that. Artemis glanced out of the window at the giant sundial below. "Wow, I really slept in, didn't I?" she said. "I was supposed to meet Apollo for archery practice ten minutes ago." She picked up her bow. "I'd better go."

"Me too," said Aphrodite. As Artemis left, she returned to her own room next door and settled on to her pillow-strewn bed to mull over the possibilities for helping Hippomenes. After reaching into her bag for her notepad and feather pen, she began a list of ideas. Before she could get very far, however, there was a knock on her door.

It was Athena. She had dressed again in the turquoise chiton Aphrodite had loaned her last night. "I'm going to the Immortal Marketplace for new knitting supplies," Athena said. "Want to come?"

"Okay," said Aphrodite, setting her pen aside. "Why not?" As they left her room, she couldn't help asking, "So did you have fun last night?"

Athena rolled her eyes. "You were lucky you left early. Those godboys wouldn't leave me alone. It was so annoying! And all because I'd had a makeover."

"Didn't I tell you?" Aphrodite couldn't help grinning. Now that Athena knew what it was like, she'd probably want to go back to being her usual self. And maybe that wouldn't be such a bad thing. Her first crush would just have to wait.

Before leaving the dorm, the girls grabbed winged sandals from the communal basket at the end of the hall and slipped them onto their feet. Immediately the sandals' straps twined around their ankles, and the silver wings at their heels began to flap. In a blur of speed, they raced down the marble staircase to the main floor of the academy. And then with their feet barely touching the ground, they zipped out of the heavy bronze doors and sped across the courtyard. The wind whistled in their ears as they whipped past boulders and trees to descend Mount Olympus.

The Immortal Marketplace stood halfway between the heavens and Earth, down below the cloud line. The two girls reached it within minutes, skidding to a stop at the entrance. Loosening the straps around their ankles, they looped them over the silver wings to hold them in place so they could walk at normal speed.

The market was enormous, with a high-ceilinged crystal roof. Rows and rows of columns separated the various shops, which sold everything from the newest Greek fashions to tridents and organic nectar.

"In here," said Athena. Aphrodite followed her into Arachne's Sewing Supplies. While Athena picked out several skeins of wool and a new pair of knitting needles, Aphrodite stroked her palm over a length of glossy black-and-red-flowered fabric that would look fabulous on Artemis with her shiny black hair. She knew better than to buy the cloth, however. Artemis would say it was too flashy.

"Let's stop at Cleo's Cosmetics," Aphrodite said as they left Arachne's. "I'm almost out of eyeliner."

"Okay," said Athena. She hesitated a moment, then added shyly, "Maybe I'll get a couple of things too."

Aphrodite arched an eyebrow in surprise.

"Nothing fancy," Athena said quickly. "Maybe just a lipstick and some of that silver eye powder you used on me last night."

"Well, what do you know?" Aphrodite said, smiling at her in amusement. But then a dark thought crossed her mind and she tensed up. Why was Athena suddenly interested in how she looked? "You've got a crush on someone, haven't you?" Aphrodite exclaimed. "Who is it?"

Athena blushed. "No one, honest. It's just that, thanks to your makeover last night, I actually felt . . .

69

well, *beautiful.*" She glanced down at her sandals, looking embarrassed. "I've never felt that way before, and . . . I kind of liked it."

Aphrodite's heart softened and she hugged her friend. "You've always been beautiful," she said. "You were just too busy inventing things and being brilliant in school to notice before now."

"Thanks," said Athena. "But the godboys didn't seem to notice before last night either."

"Only because they weren't *looking,*" said Aphrodite.

When they reached Cleo's, Aphrodite found the eyeliner she needed. Then she searched for silver eyeshadow. "Here," she said, handing Athena a little pot of the stuff. "This is the one you want."

Nodding, Athena took it and then held up a couple of lipsticks in two slightly different shades of pinkish red, one in each hand. "Which one do you think would look best on me?"

"Neither," Aphrodite said decisively. Her expert eye scanned the lipsticks on display. Snatching up an orangey-red one, she said, "This one will go best with your skin tone."

"You're the boss," said Athena, giving her a teasing smile.

"Well, Beauty-ology *is* my best subject," Aphrodite agreed. "Hey, isn't that a new assistant?"

Both goddessgirls stared at the lady behind the counter. Her purple hair was piled high on top of her head and her three eyes – two in the usual places and one in the middle of her forehead – were beautifully made up. She smiled warmly at the girls as they brought up their purchases. "Did you find everything you need?" she asked, slipping

71

the items into a small papyrus bag, then handing it to Athena.

"Yes, thank you," said Athena.

Aphrodite nodded. Then on an impulse she asked the assistant, "Are you married?"

The eye in the middle of the woman's forehead blinked. "Well, no," she said. "Why do you ask?"

"There's this teacher at MOA, Mr Cyclops. He's not married either, and I bet you'd be perfect for—"

The assistant just looked at her, blink, blink, blinking.

"Never mind her," interrupted Athena. "She's always trying to match people up. Since she's the goddessgirl of love, she can't really help it." Grabbing Aphrodite's arm, she tugged her out of the shop. "Please tell me you didn't think that assistant would be perfect for Mr Cyclops just because she has three eyes and Mr Cyclops has only one," Athena said after they were safely out of the shop.

Aphrodite grinned sheepishly. "Well, I admit it was the first thing I thought of. Also, she has lots of hair and Mr Cyclops is bald."

"So?" said Athena.

"So opposites attract," said Aphrodite. That wasn't strictly true, of course. At least not always. Still, she'd have to remember to mention the assistant to Mr Cyclops.

Athena rolled her eyes, but Aphrodite ignored her and changed the subject. "You'll never guess what happened after I got back to my room last night." She hadn't had time to tell Artemis the story, and now she was itching to share it with a girlfriend.

"Tell me," said Athena.

But just then Aphrodite spotted Ares and

Poseidon coming out of Arts of Warfare, a store that specialised in spears, tridents and thunderbolts. Casually, she steered Athena towards the boys, while at the same time pretending not to notice them. "Well, this mortal named Hippomenes sent me a message, and—"

"Hey, over here!" Ares called out when he saw them.

Both girls looked his way, and a little thrill zipped through Aphrodite as Ares drew near. But to pay him back for last night's treachery, she decided to ignore him. "Hi there, Poseidon," she said. Smiling disarmingly at him, she said the first thing that popped into her head. "I've been meaning to ask – could you tell me more about the waterworks park you designed for our last big project in Hero-ology?"

"Of course," said Poseidon, looking pleased. But

as he launched into a description of all its fabulous features, Aphrodite only half listened. To her distress, Ares didn't even seem to care that he was being ignored. Instead, he struck up a conversation with Athena.

"I like your chiton," Aphrodite heard him say. "Is it new?" How like him not to remember it was the same one Athena had worn last night.

"Thanks," Athena replied. She didn't mention that he'd already seen it on her. "It's Aphrodite's. She's letting me borrow it."

"Well, don't tell her I said so," said Ares, in a voice loud enough for Aphrodite to hear, "but I bet it looks better on you than on her."

"No it doesn't!" Athena glanced hastily towards Aphrodite.

It was nice of her friend to stick up for her, but

that didn't stop a lump from rising in Aphrodite's throat. How could Ares say such a hurtful thing? Pretending she hadn't overheard, she kept talking to Poseidon. But after a minute she turned to Athena and said, "You know? I think I'm all shopped out. Mind if we head home?"

"Not at all," said Athena. She seemed to sense Aphrodite's distress.

They bid the boys a hasty goodbye. Grabbing Athena's hand, Aphrodite pulled her away.

"See ya, Theeny," Ares called after them.

"Ares is a creep," Athena announced, as they exited the marketplace. But Aphrodite said nothing as they bent to loosen the ties on their sandals to free their silver wings. Athena glanced at her. "I know you heard what he said, but it's not true."

Aphrodite managed a small shrug. "It doesn't

matter," she lied. She was on the verge of tears and just wanted to get home to her room so she could have a good cry. The ties twined around their ankles again and the wings at their heels began to flap. They were quiet as their sandals whisked them to the top of Mount Olympus.

"I've been thinking," said Athena when they skidded to a stop before the bronze doors of the academy. "Ares was probably just trying to make you jealous. You know how much he likes to stir up trouble."

*Of course!* thought Aphrodite in relief. She should have thought of that too. "Maybe you're right." It would be just like Ares to try and beat her at her own game. He'd ignored her and pretended to be interested in Athena, just as she'd ignored him and spoken to Poseidon instead.

Slipping off their sandals, the girls walked across the main hall and up the marble stairs to the fourth floor. The marble felt cool and smooth against Aphrodite's bare feet. As the girls dropped their sandals in the fourth-floor basket, Athena pointed down the hallway to a huge bouquet of pink roses sitting right outside one of the doors. "Look! Aren't those in front of your room?"

"Yeah!" said Aphrodite, feeling a surge of excitement. Had Ares sent her flowers? Maybe he'd ordered them as an apology earlier this morning, or just now as soon as the girls had left the marketplace.

They raced to Aphrodite's door. The beautiful roses were arranged in a pottery vase painted with a black silhouette of a man in a winged chariot, the symbol for Hermes's Floral Delivery. Eagerly,

Aphrodite unrolled the small piece of papyrus attached by a ribbon to one of the blooms.

"Who're they from?" Athena asked, sounding excited for her.

Aphrodite's smile faded. "Hephaestus," she said, unable to keep the disappointment from her voice. She'd so hoped they were from Ares.

"Oh," said Athena. She hesitated. "That's nice."

Aphrodite nodded, but without enthusiasm.

"Hey, do you want to finish telling me about that message you got from a mortal last night?" Athena asked. "What was that all about?"

"Later," Aphrodite said, her shoulders slumping.

"Oh, okay," said Athena, finally seeming to sense her need to be alone. "Guess I'll go and study then. See you later."

"Okay." Aphrodite carried the roses into her room

and set them on her desk. She had to admit they were beautiful and smelled sweet. There was no real reason not to enjoy them, regardless of who had sent them. Only now she'd have to work out how to deal with Hephaestus. She didn't want him to have a crush on her! He was a nice godboy, just not her type. She hoped she could let him down gently.

Ares was another matter.

# 6

## Gossip

Aphrodite stayed in her room all day on Sunday. By staying inside, she avoided seeing Hephaestus and Ares and so avoided having to do anything about them. Instead, she sat at her desk with her red feather pen and a stack of pink papyrus and brainstormed ways to help Hippomenes. The race was the day after tomorrow!

She could slip him a pair of winged sandals, she thought, jotting down the idea. No matter how fast Atalanta was, there was no way she could win against an opponent wearing those. But the sandals' wings would be obvious to everyone. Besides, he'd have to be holding an immortal's hand to make them work properly. She doubted the king would allow anyone to race with such an advantage.

Sighing, Aphrodite crossed out the sandal idea. Maybe Hippomenes should forget about the race and just *elope* with Atalanta, she thought. If she liked him as much as Aphrodite suspected she did, she might agree. They could leave at night and be far away from the palace before the king even noticed they were missing.

But then Aphrodite remembered how she'd suggested the same strategy to Paris and Helen and caused a war! She crossed out that idea too. She worked for several hours, but every idea she came up with seemed fatally flawed. In the end, all she had to show for her efforts was a stack of paper with crossed-out sentences.

As Aphrodite entered her Hero-ology lesson the next morning, students were buzzing about something. They stopped talking as she took her seat though, eyeing her curiously. Weird. She was used to the stares of godboys, but today the goddessgirls were studying her too. There was something in their looks she couldn't quite interpret, and it made her a little nervous.

She glanced across the aisle at Athena, but as usual her nose was buried in a textscroll. Aphrodite had knocked on her door yesterday evening, intending to tell her about Hippomenes and to ask for help with ideas, but Athena had been out. Artemis too, probably walking her dogs.

Pheme coughed, as if trying to get someone's attention. When Aphrodite turned to look at her, she ducked her spiky orange head. Had she been spreading gossip again? It was to be expected, of course. She *was* the goddess of gossip and rumour, after all.

*Hmm*, thought Aphrodite, *maybe Pheme and the herald would be a good match*. Although it was true that opposites often did attract, it was good to have *some* similar interests. And weren't Pheme and the herald both in the business of announcing things? She took out her red feather pen to make a note of the idea, but then paused with her pen in mid-air. What had Pheme been announcing, she suddenly wondered?

Could it be that the gossip had been about *her?* Aphrodite's throat tightened.

Medusa's snaky head writhed and hissed as she leaned across the aisle. "Interesting weekend, Bubbles?" she asked with a smirk.

Faking a calm she didn't feel, but which had nothing to do with the snakes, Aphrodite said, "Yes, I heard you got a bit wet."

"And I heard you got a new boyfriend," Medusa shot back.

Aphrodite's eyes widened. "What are you talking about?"

Medusa smirked again as several snakes twined loosely around her neck to form a thick, live green necklace. "Pink roses?"

Aphrodite felt her cheeks grow warm.

On the other side of Medusa, Pheme giggled

nervously. So that's what she'd been gossiping about. Had *she* told Medusa about the flowers? But how could Pheme have known about them unless ... Aphrodite glanced at Athena, who was staring at Pheme with a frown on her face.

No, Athena would never tell. She was no gossip! "Yes, I got some roses. From a friend. What of it?" Aphrodite told Medusa in what she desperately hoped was a casual tone.

Medusa raised a dark green eyebrow. "Boys don't usually give roses to girls who are just friends."

"Is that right?" Aphrodite eyed her coolly. "And how would you know?"

Flicking their tongues, the snakes darted towards her as Medusa shot her a look. Good thing she wasn't mortal. She would've turned to stone at once.

Fortunately, Mr Cyclops chose that moment to begin the lesson.

When the lesson was finally over, Athena disappeared down the hall before Aphrodite could question her. But that wasn't unusual. She was always in a hurry to get to her lessons early. There was nothing she liked more than learning.

While piecing together a mosaic of the Minotaur during her next lesson, Craft-ology, Aphrodite's stomach churned as she pondered what Medusa had said. Had Athena gossiped? Of course, Aphrodite hadn't *asked* her to keep the roses a secret. But a true friend wouldn't need to be told! Distracted, Aphrodite glued several ceramic tiles in the wrong places, so that the Minotaur ended up with a horn in the middle of his chest.

When she noticed the error, she grumpily pried

up the tiles and started again. She couldn't keep her mind from wandering, however. The idea of having her name romantically linked to anyone – especially Hephaestus – was just so embarrassing. How dare he give her flowers, she thought, slapping a new tile into place. He should've known the rumours they'd cause! And how could Athena betray her confidence when she'd done so much to help her?

As the morning wore on, Aphrodite grew more and more annoyed. Paranoid, too. Whenever she heard someone whispering, she worried it might be about her and Hephaestus. At lunchtime she growled at the first godboy who offered her a place in the queue in the cafeteria. By the time she finally sat down by Persephone and Artemis, she was steaming. She slammed her bowl of Underworld stew down so hard that gravy sloshed on to the table.

The two goddessgirls glanced up in surprise. "Got it!" Artemis yelled. She grabbed three pieces of bread to soak up the gravy, then fed them to her dogs below the table. They gulped down the soppy treats without even chewing.

"Bad day?" Persephone asked sympathetically.

Aphrodite nodded. "Horrible."

Moments later, Athena dropped a bag of scrolls and a bowl of pomegranola on to the table and sat next to Aphrodite. She seemed to notice immediately that something was wrong. "What's up?" she asked.

Aphrodite just stared into her stew, fuming.

Athena looked at Artemis and Persephone, who both shrugged as if to say they didn't know what was wrong with her either.

Finally Aphrodite said, "Didn't you hear Medusa in class?"

"Oh, that." Athena dipped a spoon into her bowl. "I'd ignore her if I were you."

"Easy for you to say." Aphrodite glowered at her. "You're not the one Pheme's spreading stories about."

Athena's eyebrows rose as she lay down her spoon. "You can't think that's *my* fault."

"Well, isn't it?"

"Hold on," interrupted Persephone. "What's this all about?"

Athena sighed. "Pheme told everyone in our first lesson that someone sent Aphrodite pink roses."

"And you must've told *her*!" Aphrodite exclaimed. "How else could she have known?"

Athena stiffened. "I didn't tell. The flowers were

90

sitting outside your door, remember? Anyone could've seen them there."

"Yeah, I heard about those roses from someone in my archery lesson," Artemis said. "So which one of your many admirers sent them?"

A blush crept up Aphrodite's neck to her cheeks. "Hephaestus," she said in a low voice.

"Wasn't he talking to you at the party on Friday night?" Persephone asked.

Before Aphrodite could reply, Artemis said, "Did Medusa know the flowers were from him?"

"Even if she did, anyone could've unrolled the note attached to the flowers," Athena pointed out. "Pheme's so nosy, I wouldn't put it past her to snoop. And she does live at the end of our hall."

Athena was right, of course, thought Aphrodite. She tried to remember if Medusa had mentioned

Hephaestus's name. Maybe she *didn't* know. She was just about to apologise to Athena when Ares came up to their table.

Forgetting her plan to ignore him, Aphrodite smiled right at him. It was the kind of smile that had never failed to dazzle him – or any other godboy she'd shone it on – in the past. Only this time Ares seemed immune to her charms. "Hey, Theeny," he said, hefting Athena's bag from the table. "Can I help you carry this to your next lesson?"

Athena tugged the bag away from him and set it on the other side of her tray, out of his reach. "No thanks. I can manage."

Glancing at Persephone and Artemis, Aphrodite cringed at the looks of pity on their faces. She was sure they knew that she liked Ares a lot more than she let on. How dare they feel sorry for her!

Straightening her spine, Aphrodite said, "Don't be silly, Athena. Let him carry your scrolls. He's as strong as an ox–"

"Thanks," interrupted Ares. Grinning, he bent one arm, flexing a muscle.

"And twice as dumb as one," Aphrodite finished scornfully.

Ares winced as if she'd struck him across the face. She could feel her friends glancing at her in surprise. She knew she was being unforgivably rude, but it was too late. The words couldn't be taken back.

"Heard about your pink roses, Aphrodite," he said, loud enough for half the cafeteria to hear. "You may be the goddessgirl of love, but everyone knows you have no heart. I pity the godboy who sent them."

If everyone thought that, they were wrong,

thought Aphrodite, blinking back sudden tears. She did have a heart, and it felt like he'd just stomped on it!

"You'd never catch me sending flowers," Ares continued. "It's such a *girly* thing to do."

"Shut up, Ares," said Artemis.

"Maybe you should just go," Persephone suggested to him. "Now's a bad time."

Abruptly, Athena stood. "No. I'm going," she said. She reached for her bag, but Ares tugged it away from her.

"I'll carry it," he said. "Please? I want to talk to you about something."

After a moment of hesitation, Athena gave in and the two of them left together.

Aphrodite stood too. Glancing at Persephone and Artemis's faces, she muttered, "Stop looking at me like that. I don't care if he likes her. In fact, he can marry her for all I care!" Then, just like at the party, she fled the room, her cheeks burning and her heart broken.

# 7

# The Olive Grove

Somehow Aphrodite got through the rest of the day. She was glad none of her friends were in her afternoon classes. She knew she'd behaved badly at lunch and didn't want to face them quite yet. Instead of returning to her room after school, she stowed her textscrolls in her locker and headed outside.

"Aphrodite, wait up!"

*Hephaestus!* Had he been hanging around waiting for her? She was in no mood to talk to him – or any godboy – right now. She pretended not to hear him and raced across the courtyard, thinking she could easily outdistance him.

But Hephaestus just kept calling. Aphrodite could hear his cane thumping along behind her more quickly than she would have thought possible. She didn't want to be mean, but couldn't he take a hint? She wanted to be alone! Afraid someone would hear him calling to her – someone like Pheme or Medusa – she finally looked around for a private place to talk to him, somewhere that no one would see them together.

To one side of the courtyard there was a grove of olive trees that would offer some shelter from prying eyes. Waving to Hephaestus to follow, Aphrodite headed towards it. The park of silver-green trees had only sprung up recently – a result of Athena's invention of the olive.

"Whoa. You sure walk fast," said Hephaestus as he finally caught up with her. Breathing hard, he leaned against the trunk of a tree, causing some of its silver-green leaves to flutter to the ground. "Did you get the roses I sent?"

"Yes, thank you," said Aphrodite, sitting cross-legged on the stone bench under another tree. Now that they were face to face, she realised it wasn't going to be easy to tell him she didn't like him – not as a boyfriend, that is. She took a deep breath. "But you really shouldn't have–"

"Sent them?" interrupted Hephaestus. He pushed off the trunk of the tree and came to sit beside her. "I hope they didn't give you the wrong idea."

"Well . . . " Aphrodite began uncertainly.

Before she could say another word, Hephaestus forced a chuckle. "There's a rumour going around that you've got a new boyfriend. It would be stupid if everyone thought it was me, huh? I mean, is there a law that says you can't give flowers to a friend?"

His face was so earnest that she heard herself say, "No law that I know of."

Hephaestus hesitated and she felt him glance at her, then away. "So, did you like the . . . " he cleared his throat. ". . . The roses?"

"They're very pretty." She paused. "And they smell great. Sweet. Just like the godboy who gave them to me, but . . . "

Hephaestus cut her off, speaking enthusiastically.

"Was I right to guess that pink is your favourite colour? You wear it a lot."

"I love pink," said Aphrodite. She smiled fondly at him.

"What?" he asked, reading something in her expression.

She shrugged. "I was just thinking that you're so different from the other godboys."

He straightened, looking insulted.

"That's a compliment," she said quickly. "I mean, I can't think of even one other godboy perceptive enough to notice how much pink I wear and to realise it's my favourite colour." Certainly Ares wouldn't. Given the way he'd been treating her recently, it was a mystery that she still liked the guy. But then the workings of the heart *were* mysterious.

Hephaestus smiled shyly and then pulled

100

something from his pocket. "I have another gift for you."

"Oh, Hephaestus, no," Aphrodite began, holding up both palms to stop him. But ignoring her protest, he slipped a wide gold bracelet on her wrist. "Ooh, it's gorgeous!" she exclaimed, twisting the bracelet back and forth on her wrist so it glinted in the sun that filtered through the trees. The bracelet had been hammered thin, then etched with a delicate-looking leaf pattern. In between the leaves were tiny roses of a pink-tinted precious metal known as rose gold.

"Thanks," said Hephaestus, his delight obvious.

"Where did you get it? The jewellery shop in the Immortal Marketplace?" It was so lovely, she couldn't take her eyes from it. But of course, she had to give it back. Didn't she?

"I made it," Hephaestus said, smiling proudly. "For you."

"Oh, Hephaestus, you're really talented. But I'm not sure ..." Aphrodite hesitated, toying with the bracelet some more. She really wanted to keep it, but she didn't want to give him the wrong idea. If she accepted it, wouldn't he think she wanted to be his girlfriend?

Just then a twig snapped nearby, startling them both. Someone else had entered the grove. "Quick – hide!" Aphrodite whispered. "We can't let anyone see us together!"

A look of hurt crossed Hephaestus's face, but then his expression turned wooden and he nodded. "Of course, I understand. I'll go." Rising to his feet with the help of his silver cane, he took a step away. Then he paused and turned back. For just a second, he looked at her without saying anything. Aphrodite realised he was probably waiting for her to change her mind, to say, *Who cares what people think? Let them see us together.* At the sweet hope in his eyes, she almost did change her mind. But then the trees shifted just a bit and she saw who had entered the grove.

*Ares!* Against her will, her heart began to beat fast. "See you later, Hephaestus!" she said hurriedly, waving him on his way.

With his shoulders slumped, he left.

Aphrodite shoved aside her guilty feelings for the way she'd treated him and spread the skirt of her chiton on the bench seat so it draped gracefully on either side of her. When Ares noticed her, she'd act surprised, as if she hadn't heard him approaching. He was probably coming to say he was sorry for ignoring her these past few days and for saying she had no heart. If he apologised nicely, she might just find it in her heart – the heart he was sure didn't exist – to apologise for comparing his intelligence to that of an ox.

"Yuck! It tastes terrible!" Ares spat something out. "How can mortals like these things?"

Startled, Aphrodite stiffened. Ares wasn't alone! Who was he speaking to?

She almost fell off the bench when she heard a familiar voice reply, "You can't eat olives right off the tree. They have to cure first."

*Athena?* Jealousy surged through Aphrodite like a rushing river. What was she up to, coming here with Ares? She didn't even *like* him! Or did she?

Quickly, Aphrodite turned herself into a lovebird and flew high into the branches of the closest olive

104

tree, planning to spy and find out once and for all. Her heart thumped fast inside her feathered breast when Ares and Athena came into view.

"That explains it," said Ares, holding back a branch so Athena could pass. "I knew you couldn't have invented something that tastes so bitter."

Aphrodite's beady eyes blinked in surprise. It was the kind of flirtatious line Ares had once used on *her*.

"The Greeks have found all kinds of uses for my olive," said Athena, pride in her voice. "They're not just eating them. They're also squeezing oil from them to burn in their lamps and to heat their homes. They're even making perfume and medicine from them."

*Keep it up*, Aphrodite thought jealously. If she knew Ares like she thought she did, he'd soon grow bored. A godboy of action, he'd always had little patience for what he called "goddessgirl prattle".

But Ares shocked her by saying, "You know, I've never met a girl as smart as you, Athena. It's so refreshing."

*Refreshing?* What was that supposed to mean? The remark really ruffled Aphrodite's feathers. Was Ares implying that she was dumb? Beautiful, but dumb? She felt annoyed enough to peck out his eyes!

Sounding flustered, Athena squeaked, "Really?"

"Honest," said Ares. He picked several olives and began juggling them. "You'd *have* to be smart to have a town named after you. It's called Athens, right? Who would've thought your invention of the olive would win you such an amazing honour?"

Athena shrugged modestly. "Yeah, well, it was a surprise to me, too."

"Really impressive," Ares murmured as if he hadn't heard her. "I wouldn't mind having a city named after *me*."

*No surprise there*, thought Aphrodite. Ares's ego was bigger than Colossus. Why *did* she waste her time on him? As the goddessgirl of love, you'd think that matters of the heart would be transparent to her. But when it came to her own love life, she was as clueless as anyone else – mortal or immortal. Ares *was* awfully handsome, though, and he could be charming. When he'd danced her around the gym at the Harvest Hop a few weeks ago, he'd had eyes only for her as he twirled her expertly across the floor. Lost in memory, she missed the next few things Athena and Ares said to each other.

She was jerked back to the present when Athena suddenly stood up. "Get lost!"

"Aww, Theeny," Ares pleaded, rising too. "Don't be mad. You know I didn't mean it like that."

Aphrodite scolded herself for not paying better attention. What had she missed?

Athena's back stiffened. "And don't call me Theeny! Only my dad calls me that."

Throwing his hands up, Ares muttered, "Sorry!"

"Just go." Athena turned her back on him.

Ares sighed. "All right, but think about what I asked, okay?" He leaned closer to Athena, but she ducked away. Frowning, he said, "Fine. But don't think I'm giving up."

After Ares left, Athena sunk to the ground and began to sob. Aphrodite was shocked. She'd never seen her friend cry before. Instantly, her jealousy vanished, washed away in the flood of Athena's tears. Fluttering down from her tree, she changed back into a goddess.

"Where did you come from?" Athena asked, jumping to her feet. She swiped at her wet eyes with the back of her hand. Aphrodite pointed to the tree behind her. Athena's cheeks reddened. "You were spying?"

"No, it wasn't like that, I—" But before Aphrodite could explain, Athena gave a strangled cry.

"You planned this with Ares as some sort of test, didn't you? I thought you were my friend, but ... " Shaking her head, Athena backed away. Then she turned and ran from the grove.

Aphrodite stared after her, upset and totally confused. *Planned what? What test?* She had no idea what Athena could possibly have meant by that.

# 8

# An Argument

Aphrodite hurried across the courtyard to go after Athena. She was halfway there when she spied Pheme's spiky orange head amid a group of godboys and goddessgirls. Aphrodite crouched low, hoping to sneak past her.

Unfortunately, Pheme had already spotted her, and she rushed over. "I just saw Athena," she said, her words puffing from her lips like miniature smoke writing. "She seemed awfully upset about something. Any idea what?"

"Not a clue," lied Aphrodite. She wasn't about to give Pheme any new gossip to repeat. "See you later. I've got homework." With a wave of her hand, she plunged on ahead.

"Wait!" Pheme caught up with her at the bottom of the school's granite steps and clutched her wrist. Hephaestus's gift sparkled in the sunlight. "Where did you get this beautiful bracelet?"

Aphrodite jerked her arm away and hid it behind her back. "It was a gift," she mumbled. "From a friend."

Pheme licked her orange-glossed lips eagerly. "More like from an *admirer*, I'm guessing. Want to tell me his name?"

"Not a chance," Aphrodite said stiffly.

Pheme cocked her head. "Then I guess I'll have to draw my own conclusions."

"You always do," Aphrodite muttered. Turning, she raced up the steps to the school. But once she reached Athena's door, she hesitated. Maybe she should give her friend a few minutes to cool off? Entering her own room, she saw the turquoise chiton she'd let Athena borrow balled up on her bed. She must've returned it as soon as she'd got back to her room.

Irritation welled up in Aphrodite as she shook out the chiton and saw how wrinkled it was. As she was smoothing it, she was annoyed to notice a tiny rip under its arm and a faint stain near the hem. The least Athena could have done was wash it before returning it.

Suddenly, Aphrodite didn't feel sorry for her any more. Grabbing the chiton, she marched up the hallway with it and knocked sharply on Athena's door. Then, without waiting for her to answer, she thrust it open.

Athena was alone, sitting at her desk, her blue Beauty-ology textscroll open before her. "Well, just come on in," she grumped.

"Look!" Aphrodite shook out the chiton and jabbed a finger at the stain near the hem. "You ruined it!"

Athena rolled her eyes. "It'll wash out."

"Oh yeah?" Aphrodite frowned. Athena obviously didn't think how she treated other people's things was important. "Well, this won't wash out!" She pointed to the rip under the arm.

Athena squinted at the hole. "I'm sorry, but really,

that hole is so tiny I didn't even notice it. No one else will either."

"But *I'll* know it's there!" Aphrodite exclaimed. She wouldn't be able to wear the chiton again without worrying that someone would see the rip.

"I said I was sorry," Athena said with a frown. "Maybe you shouldn't have lent me your chiton if you were so afraid I'd ruin it. It wasn't *my* idea to get dressed up and go to that party!"

"Oh, really?" Aphrodite huffed. "Well, you certainly seemed to enjoy yourself once you were there, with all those godboys hanging on your every word."

Athena blinked, looking shocked. "You're jealous? Of me? I thought you hated all the attention you get from those godboys."

"That's not the point!" Aphrodite snapped in confusion.

Athena rocked back in her chair. "Then what is?"

"I – I don't know!" Aphrodite exclaimed. Suddenly, all the fight drained out of her. She sagged against the edge of Athena's desk. She didn't really care about the chiton – she had *dozens* of them. Athena was right, she *was* jealous, and it was time to set things straight.

"Listen." Aphrodite took a deep breath. "Back in the olive grove? I was telling the truth. I really *didn't* follow you. I was there before you – with someone."

"Oh," said Athena, her eyes round with surprise. "Hephaestus?" she guessed.

Aphrodite nodded. "When we heard someone coming, I made him leave. I wanted to be with Ares. But when I saw you'd come with him, I hid. I didn't mean to spy. It just happened."

"Ares doesn't like me, you know," Athena said

115

quietly. "He never really did. It's like you said: just because a boy fusses over you, it doesn't mean he's in love with you."

Aphrodite blinked. She had said that, hadn't she? But it wasn't always true. "What do you mean? He's been ignoring me since the party. He only wants to talk to you!"

Athena shook her head. "He was never interested in me. He just heard about Athens and everything, and he wanted me to ask my dad to name a city on Earth after *him*." She paused. "I honestly thought you knew. I thought maybe Ares had talked to you, and together you'd come up with a plan for how he could get me to do what he wanted."

Aphrodite drew in her breath. "I'd never do that to you," she said. "But that sounds like Ares, all right!" Now that she thought about it, she remembered him telling Athena that he wouldn't mind having a city named after him. *Humph.* Ares hadn't been very nice to Athena. Or to *her*, for that matter. But had *she* treated Hephaestus any better? she wondered guiltily. In their own ways, she and Ares had both behaved badly. Why did relationships between godboys and goddessgirls have to be so complicated?

"You know," Athena said thoughtfully, "I was perfectly happy before the makeover. And I'm not really interested in having a boyfriend – at least not right now. I agreed to the makeover only because I thought I could learn something from it that would help me out in Beauty-ology." She looked down at her lap. "I'm not doing so well in that class."

"Really?" Aphrodite put a hand on Athena's

shoulder to comfort her. She almost sounded as if she were going to cry again.

"I got a B-plus on my project in Beauty-ology!" Athena blurted.

"Is that bad?" Aphrodite asked uncertainly.

"Are you kidding? It's my first B-plus ever!" Athena sounded devastated. "I've never even had as low as an A-minus before!"

"Oh," Aphrodite said, surprised. Then she remembered all the times she'd seen Athena studying the blue Beauty-ology scroll lately, and the questions she'd asked about different cosmetics, clothing and hairstyles. Beauty-ology was second nature to Aphrodite. She'd excelled in it every term since the first year. She'd never considered that the class might be difficult for someone who wasn't as well versed in the subject as she was.

"Do you need some help with your homework?" Aphrodite offered.

Athena looked hopeful. "Really?"

"Of course, what are friends for?"

Athena smiled at her. "Thanks. And I'm sorry about your chiton. I'll buy you a new one."

"You keep it." Aphrodite waved her hand dismissively. "I've got more chitons than I can ever wear. Besides, Ares was right about one thing. It *does* look better on you than on me."

Catching sight of the bracelet on Aphrodite's wrist, Athena exclaimed, "Ooh! That's gorgeous! Where did you get it?"

Aphrodite rubbed a finger over the engraved rosebuds. "Hephaestus gave it to me," she confessed. "I shouldn't have accepted it, though. I'm going to give it back."

"But it's so beautiful," Athena protested.

"Yes," said Aphrodite, "but it would be wrong to keep it. I'm pretty sure he gave it to me because he's hoping I'll be his girlfriend."

Athena frowned in genuine confusion. "So a girl has to like a boy as more than a friend, just because he gives her a gift?"

"Not always," said Aphrodite, amused. Boy–girl relationships might baffle her sometimes, but it was obvious that Athena knew far less than *she* did! "It kind of depends on the boy and the gift."

Athena eyed the bracelet longingly. "Well, *I'd* be tempted to keep it. Any girl would – mortal or immortal."

At her words, something clicked in Aphrodite's brain. "That's it!" she exclaimed. "I know how to help Hippomenes win his race!"

# 9

## The Race

"Atalanta – I've heard about that maiden," Athena said when Aphrodite finished telling her all about Hippomenes and Atalanta and the plan she'd just come up with to help them. "Her fame as a runner is all over the school." She paused. "Are you sure she wants to marry your Hippomenes?"

"Definitely," said Aphrodite, remembering Atalanta's tears.

"But where are you going to find apples made of gold by tomorrow?" asked Athena. "I've never seen any around here."

Aphrodite grinned. "I'm going to ask Hephaestus for help."

Not long afterwards, she tracked him down as he was leaving the cafeteria. "Hephaestus. Wait up!" she called to him. Even though she'd been rude in the grove, he still smiled broadly when he saw her, and waited near the door. When she caught up with him, she slipped the gold bracelet off her wrist. "I've decided I can't keep it after all," she said apologetically. "But thanks for letting me borrow it."

His face fell as he took the bracelet from her. She

could tell he was trying hard to hide his hurt feelings. "No problem."

Aphrodite felt terrible. But it wasn't her fault that her heart didn't beat for Hephaestus. She smiled brightly, hoping to cheer him up. "It's so beautiful I didn't want to give it up. But you should keep it. Some day you might want to give it to your future wife." She sat down on a bench in the hallway outside the cafeteria and motioned for him to sit beside her.

"But I was hoping a girlfriend might want to wear it in the meantime," he said softly.

Aphrodite gulped. Poor Hephaestus. He was probably the nicest godboy she knew. In an effort to comfort him, she said, "Don't worry. I'm certain the right goddessgirl will come along soon." She could only hope she spoke the truth. Then it dawned on her. She could *help* him find just the right girl. But first things first. Changing the subject, she said, "Hippomenes's race is tomorrow. You said I should ask if there was anything you could do to help." She paused. "Is your offer still open?"

"Of course," Hephaestus said readily.

She told him her plan.

"That's brilliant," he said. "How many apples do you want me to make?"

"Three should do the trick," said Aphrodite. "I hope so anyway."

Hephaestus nodded, then rose from the bench. "I'll get started now. That way they'll be ready for you first thing tomorrow morning."

"Thanks." She stood and gave him a hug. "You're a true friend."

He smiled at her, turning a little pink. "I guess I can settle for that."

Aphrodite returned his smile. She hoped she could find a goddessgirl worthy of him!

Later that evening, Aphrodite returned to Athena's room to help her with a Beauty-ology project. Using ground almonds, oats, yogurt and crushed, dry lavender, they concocted a refreshing facial scrub. The two girls had just applied the resulting paste to their faces and throats when Artemis and Persephone came by.

"Godness!" Persephone shrieked, her pale face turning even paler than usual when Athena opened her door. "What's happened to you?"

When Aphrodite appeared in the doorway too, Artemis laughed. "Maybe I should get a doctor. Whatever Athena's got, it seems to be contagious."

"It's a facial mask. Want to try it?" Athena asked. "It feels great."

Soon all four girls had goop on their faces. "Good thing my dogs are in my room," said Artemis. "This stuff smells so good, they'd go crazy trying to lick it off." After rubbing the paste in with soft cloths, they waited twenty minutes, then trooped down to the hall bathroom to rinse it off.

When they returned to Athena's room, Aphrodite told Persephone and Artemis about Hippomenes too. "It would be great if you'd all come with me to the race tomorrow," she said. "It's early enough that we should have time to get back before our lessons start."

Athena looked up from her desk, where she'd been scribbling down the facial scrub recipe while Aphrodite recounted her story again. "I'll come," she said.

"Me too," echoed Persephone.

"Wouldn't miss it for the world," said Artemis. "I'll bring my dogs, too."

Hippomenes's eyes widened when he saw all four goddesses approaching the deserted sandy racecourse at dawn the next morning. Aphrodite introduced him to her friends. "Down, boys!" shouted Artemis when her hounds leaped up on him.

"That's okay," said Hippomenes, rubbing Amby under the chin. "We've met once before, so that makes us old friends."

From the bag she'd brought, Aphrodite pulled out the three golden apples Hephaestus had made. She'd asked him to come too, but he'd stayed up late to make the apples and had some homework he needed to finish before his first lesson.

The apples were perfectly round and polished to a high golden shine. Hephaestus had used all his skills as a metalsmith to craft them. Just like the bracelet, they were so irresistible that Aphrodite wished she could keep them herself. But after a moment's hesitation, she dropped the apples into Hippomenes's cupped hands.

"What do I do with these?" he asked.

"Keep them with you during the race," she told him. "You'll work out how to use them when the time is right." More than that she would not tell him. He needed to be wise enough to puzzle some things out for himself.

"Thank you, O Wonderful and Beautiful Goddess," said Hippomenes, bowing. "I hope to prove worthy of your help."

As a throng of people began gathering to watch

the race, Aphrodite and her friends melted into the crowd. Minutes later, golden-haired Atalanta appeared, accompanied by her father, King Schoeneus.

After a few moments she left the king and joined Hippomenes at the starting line. Glancing at him with tender eyes filled with sadness, Atalanta crouched beside him, waiting for the signal to begin the race. Seconds later, the trumpets sounded and they were off.

"Go, Hippomenes!" shouted the four goddessgirls.

At first he held his own, managing to race side by side with Atalanta, but after a while she began pulling ahead. Swift as a chariot, she sped further and further away.

"Faster, Hippomenes!" yelled the goddessgirls. Their voices blended together with those of the crowd, which was also urging the youth on. Squeezing her hands together, Aphrodite willed him to think of the apples. At that moment, Atalanta glanced over her shoulder to check on Hippomenes's speed. The action caused her to slow a little, and in that instant Hippomenes's face lit up as if an idea had struck him. Drawing the first apple from his sash, he threw it into the air so that it rolled on to the track just ahead of Atalanta.

Transfixed by its shiny goldness, the girl hesitated, then bent to scoop it up. As she did so, Hippomenes dashed past her.

The crowd cheered, and the goddessgirls pumped their fists in the air. "Way to go, Hippomenes!" shouted Aphrodite. Pocketing the first apple, Atalanta soon caught up and passed him again. Reaching into his sash, Hippomenes drew out the second apple and flung it with all his might. It glinted in the morning sun as it rolled in front of Atalanta and came to rest at the edge of the track. As she darted over to pick it up, Hippomenes passed her once more.

By now the goal marks were in sight. But as before, Atalanta quickly drew even with Hippomenes, then pulled ahead in a fresh burst of speed. "Oh no!" cried Aphrodite. Poor Hippomenes was breathing heavily, his sides heaving. But with his last bit of strength, he hurled the final golden apple. It struck the course at Atalanta's feet and bounced wide. Unable to resist, she swerved to follow. As she stooped to capture it, Hippomenes stumbled across the finish line.

A shout went up from the crowd, and just like the mortals around them, the goddessgirls jumped for joy and hugged one another. Hippomenes sent Aphrodite a wave of thanks as he trotted to a small stage that had been set up near the track. She smiled, waving back.

A palace attendant placed a wreath on Hippomenes's head, and Atalanta came to stand beside him. Smiling broadly, she held up the golden apples for all to see. "Hippomenes has won," she proclaimed loudly. "I am glad to give up the race, and that it is he who has won this victory from me."

"I will only count myself the true winner," said Hippomenes, gazing at her lovingly, "if you say I've won your heart."

Atalanta blushed. "And so you have."

The goddessgirls sighed.

"How romantic." Aphrodite's eyes shone as bright as the golden apples as Atalanta took Hippomenes's hand and led him to the king, who would soon be blessing their marriage. It felt good to have played a part in bringing the two young mortals together.

"Ye gods!" Athena exclaimed. "If we don't hurry back, we'll be late to class!" The girls loosened the ties to free the silver wings at their heels. As the ties twined around their ankles, the wings began to flap. Artemis's dogs raced along behind as, within minutes, the sandals whisked all four girls up the mountainside and through the clouds to the top of Mount Olympus.

# 10

## Perfect Matches

That afternoon, at Aphrodite's invitation, Hephaestus joined the goddessgirls in the cafeteria for a snack. While sipping ambrosia shakes, the girls took turns telling him about the race.

As Persephone described the spellbound look on Atalanta's face when she glimpsed the first golden apple, Aphrodite noticed a goddessgirl with curly brown hair watching them from several tables away. There was a dreamy expression on her face as her pretty brown eyes settled on Hephaestus – the kind of expression Aphrodite often saw on her *own* admirers' faces. The girl looked away when she saw she'd been noticed gaping at him. "Do you know that goddessgirl?" Aphrodite interrupted, looking at Hephaestus and nodding her head in the girl's direction.

He glanced towards the brown-haired girl. "Mmm. She's new here at MOA. Her name's Aglaia. She's in my Beast-ology class."

"Interesting," said Aphrodite. "She was looking at you just then."

He shrugged and turned back towards Persephone. "So then what did Hippomenes do?"

*Honestly,* thought Aphrodite, *sometimes godboys are so*

135

*dense*. "Excuse me," she said, interrupting again. "But that girl wasn't just looking at you. She was looking at you like she *likes* you."

Artemis, Persephone and Athena giggled. Blushing, Hephaestus glanced at Aglaia again, this time with a little more interest. Across the room, the new girl caught his eye. Her cheeks turned pink as she smiled shyly at him.

Aphrodite nudged him with her elbow. "Maybe you should go and talk to her. Or if you'd like, we could invite her over here. I bet she'd enjoy hearing all about how your golden apples saved the day too."

Hephaestus's eyes twinkled. "Are you trying to set me up?" He might not be handsome to her, Aphrodite thought, but there was something about the sparkle in his eyes that made him attractive nonetheless. *Inner* beauty, she realised. That's what the sparkle was.

"Of course I'm trying to set you up," she said with a grin. "I'm the goddessgirl of love, after all. That's what I do."

"Fair enough," Hephaestus said. The four goddessgirls looked at him expectantly. "All right," he said at last. "I'll go and talk to her." He took a deep breath, then stood up from the table. Shifting his weight, he leaned forward on his silver cane. "Well, here I go."

"Wait." On an impulse, Aphrodite hopped up and gave him a quick peck on the cheek.

He covered his cheek with his palm, looking pleased and surprised. "What was that for?"

"For you – for being beautiful inside and out. Okay, now you can go." She made little shooing motions with her hands as her friends giggled again.

With a look of greater confidence, Hephaestus headed towards Aglaia's table. Having witnessed the kiss, she was frowning slightly now. Never mind, thought Aphrodite. Her reputation as MOA's most beautiful and sought-after goddessgirl probably wouldn't do Hephaestus any harm.

Seconds later, a group of godboys entered the cafeteria. Ares was with them. Seeing him this time, Aphrodite's heart didn't flutter like it usually did. He might be handsome, she thought, but he seemed to lack other more important qualities – like the kindness and loyalty and generosity that Hephaestus and Hippomenes had shown.

Glimpsing the girls, Ares left his friends and swaggered over to their table. "Hey, Theeny," he said, ignoring the others. "Have you given any more thought to that thing we talked about?"

"Not at all," Athena said coolly. "And I'm not going to change my mind."

"Aw, Theeny," pleaded Ares. "Don't be that way."

"You should listen better," said Aphrodite. "As she told you before, her name's Athena, not Theeny."

Ares's head swung towards her. He smiled unkindly. "What's that, Bubbles?"

"Don't call her that!" growled Artemis. And from under the table her dogs growled too.

Persephone frowned at him. "I think you'd better leave."

"It's all right," said Aphrodite. "He probably said that without thinking—"

Ares interrupted. "Not really, I—"

139

"The way he does most things," she finished.

Her friends burst into laughter.

With a snarl, Ares turned on his heel and stalked away.

Athena scowled at his back. "He and Medusa are two of a kind."

"That's for sure," said Persephone. "They're both *bullies*."

"Talk about a perfect match," said Artemis. "Those two were made for each other."

"You are so right!" Aphrodite exclaimed. Her eyes sparkled as she said, "There've been a lot of rumours going around this week. How about we start one of our own?"

It wasn't long before the goddessgirls reassembled in Aphrodite's room. She handed Athena her red feather pen and a sheet of pink papyrus.

"What colour should the roses be?" Athena asked.

"Red," said Persephone.

Aphrodite nodded. "Most definitely red."

"The flowers of *loooove*," Artemis said teasingly.

Athena quickly wrote down the order, addressing it to Hermes's Floral Delivery. Then she rolled up the papyrus sheet and tied a piece of ribbon around it. As she chanted the Send spell, the little scroll rose from Aphrodite's desk and zoomed towards her window. "Wait!" Aphrodite cried. But it was too late. The papyrus crashed against the windowpane, crumpling, then spiralling dizzily to the floor.

"Sorry, I forgot," Aphrodite said. As the scroll slowly raised itself up, she opened the window. With what seemed like a show of dignity, the papyrus uncrumpled itself, then hopped on to the window sill. From there, it dived into the wind and was swiftly swept away.

# 11

## Red Roses

When school finished the following afternoon, Aphrodite and her friends lingered in the main hall near the marble staircase that led up to the dorms until Ares appeared. As usual, beefy Kydoimos and squinty-eyed Makhai stuck to him like bodyguards. Ares glowered at the goddessgirls as he came near, but Aphrodite smiled at him sweetly. "Hi, Ares." She turned towards Athena. "Ask him about those flowers you got," she said. "Those red roses he sent."

Kydoimos stared at Ares with a look of surprise, and Makhai raised a scornful eyebrow. "What roses?" Ares spluttered, embarrassed. "I never sent anyone roses."

"Really? They were gorgeous!" Persephone exclaimed. "And they smelled as sweet as ambrosia."

Around them, curious students paused to listen to this interesting conversation. As more and more gathered at the foot of the stairs, Aphrodite was pleased to glimpse Medusa and Pheme among them. They must have overheard because their heads were together and Pheme was whispering excitedly. It didn't seem to bother her when Medusa's snakes slithered and wound through her spiky hair. Or maybe she was just too busy gossiping to notice.

Aphrodite gazed soulfully at Ares. "A godboy could win any girl's heart with flowers like that. Right, Athena?"

Batting her eyelashes, Athena sighed theatrically. "So true."

"Well ... " he said slowly. His eyes shifted between the two girls, and Aphrodite could tell he was trying to work out how to turn things to his advantage. He was so *calculating*. Why hadn't she seen that before? "I guess maybe I *did* send those flowers," he said finally. "Glad you liked them." He gave them his most charming smile, and she felt certain he was betting that an Athena in love would change her mind about speaking to her dear old dad on his behalf.

"Oh, I did," Athena assured him. "But of course I can't keep them."

"Huh?" said Ares.

Medusa inched closer and the few mortals in the crowd shrank away or covered their eyes so as not to accidentally look at her. Cupping a hand around her ear, Pheme leaned forward too, like she didn't want to miss a single word.

"Yeah. Too bad they were delivered to you by mistake, right, Athena?" Artemis said.

"Huh?" Ares said again, looking totally confused.

"I finally checked the note you sent with them," Athena explained. Then she looked straight at Medusa. "You're one lucky girl!"

Medusa's eyes widened in surprise, but then a smile spread over her glossy green lips and she gave Ares a dreamy look. "They were for *me*?"

"What?" Red roses bloomed in Ares's cheeks and he backed up a step. "Wait a second, I never–"

"I'm sure you'll enjoy them," Aphrodite interrupted, smiling at Medusa. "What girl wouldn't!"

For a second Medusa's smile wavered. She glanced suspiciously at the four goddessgirls. So did her snakes. Frowning, she reached up to stroke one of them and it wound around her wrist, hissing affectionately. "You're not having us on, are you?" she asked.

*Us?* Was Medusa referring to herself and Pheme . . . or to herself and the *snakes*? Maybe both, thought Aphrodite. "Why would we do that?" she asked innocently.

Artemis shrugged. "If you don't want the flowers, I'm sure Athena would be happy to keep them."

Athena nodded vigorously, but Medusa still looked uncertain.

"We put the vase outside your room," Persephone said.

"Go and take a look if you don't believe us," added Athena.

Before Medusa could respond, Pheme pushed through the crowd and started upstairs. Aphrodite could bet she was making a beeline for Medusa's room. Hurrying after her, Medusa called out, "Hey, wait for me. The flowers are mine!"

The goddessgirls grinned at one another. Once Pheme saw the roses and the card they'd asked Hermes Floral Delivery to send on Ares's behalf, it wouldn't be long before Ares and Medusa's names would be paired together on everyone's lips. Ares must have realised that too, because he raced upstairs after Medusa, a worried look on his face.

Some of the students in the crowd dashed after them, wanting to see what else would happen. The rest left in groups, busily discussing the merits and drawbacks of this surprising new romance. Aphrodite sighed with pleasure. "I don't think I've ever made a more deserving match." Feeling more lighthearted than she had in days, she bent to pet Artemis's dogs, and didn't even mind when Suez slobbered on her hand.

Later, the four friends walked past the sports fields at the edge of the academy, down to the Immortal Marketplace, where they bought some snacks to share. On the way back they wove silly spells together and made sweets and crisps dance in the air. The hounds were delighted, especially Amby. Ears flapping, he leaped to snatch the treats and quickly gobbled them down.

"Anyone want to race?" Artemis asked as they came alongside the athletics field.

Persephone giggled. "Not without my winged sandals."

"Have you ever seen anyone who could run as fast as Atalanta?" Athena asked.

"Well, Ares is pretty fast," said Aphrodite.

The other girls looked at her, as if surprised she could still say something nice about him. She shrugged. "It doesn't mean I've still got a crush on him. But you know he's won the footraces in every Olympic games since Year One."

Artemis nodded. "True. But do you think *he* could beat Atalanta?"

"Maybe," Aphrodite said. Then she grinned. "Especially if Medusa was chasing him."

Laughing, the goddessgirls reached the courtyard.

As they passed a group of godboys at the base of the granite stairs, all heads turned to look at Aphrodite. "Hey!" yelled the centaur from Mr Cyclops's class, the godboy she'd made blush only a few days ago. "Will you dance with me at the school party this weekend?"

"Hold on! I was going to ask her!" Poseidon chimed in. "Me too," said another godboy.

Artemis rolled her eyes. "Looks like things are pretty much back to normal," she whispered.

"One of these days you'll find out what it's like to have a crush on someone," Persephone teased.

Athena nodded, grinning. "I'd like to see that!"

"Hey!" said Artemis, looking a little worried. "Aphrodite doesn't *need* any more matchmaking ideas."

Aphrodite cocked her head. "I might do." Then

she smiled over at the hopeful centaur. Yes, boys could be annoying, but some of them were also sweet. "I'll dance with you," she said. "Are you any good?"

The godboy grinned. "I think so." He stamped his hooves.

"Don't believe him!" Poseidon yelled. "Can't you see he's got two left feet?" The boys started laughing and began good-naturedly tussling on the ground.

Athena shook her head at their silliness. "Godboys will be godboys," she said dryly.

"You can say that again," Artemis agreed.

Persephone grinned. "You can't take the boy out of the godboy that's for sure."

"And would we really want to if we could?" asked Aphrodite. Then she called out, "See you at the dance, guys!" Her smile dazzled the entire group, leaving them all rooted to the spot with their mouths hanging open.

"Like I said, looks like things are back to normal," Artemis teased. Persephone and Athena grinned.

Aphrodite laughed. "And I wouldn't have it any other way." Linking arms with her friends, the four of them climbed the steps to the academy's front doors.

READ ON FOR A TASTER OF THE

NEXT ADVENTURE WITH THE

*Goddess Girls*

**ARTEMIS**

**THE BRAVE**

On silver-winged magic sandals, Artemis zoomed through the Forest of the Beasts, her feet gliding just a few centimetres above the mossy forest floor. "Come out, come out, wherever you are," she sing-songed under her breath.

Dodging tree trunks and ducking under low-hanging vines, she listened carefully for any unusual sounds. Her keen dark eyes searched the dense woods. Her favourite bow – its limbs made of curved, polished olive wood – was at the ready. A tooled leather quiver of arrows was slung across her back. She could pull one out and have it nocked and aimed in a split second, as soon as it was needed.

Behind her, Artemis heard Athena whizzing along

in winged sandals as well. And following her were Aphrodite and Persephone. All four goddessgirls wore ankle-length flowing gowns called chitons, and their skirts whipped in the breeze as they zipped through the forest of olive, fig and pomegranate trees, their feet never quite touching the ground.

They had come here this afternoon for one purpose: to duel with some of the slimiest, smelliest beasts ever to roam the Earth. Armed with magic-tipped arrows, the goddessgirls had already defeated a she-dragon called Echidna and beaten a goat-headed Chimera. Now they had only ten minutes left to find the third beast they were tracking.

Winning this one final battle of good versus evil was critical. Something very important hung in the balance.

Their grades.

On the first Friday of every month, all the goddessgirls and godboys in their Beast-ology class left Mount Olympus Academy and came down to Earth. Here in this forest, for an entire hour, they played games of skill that Professor Ladon had created to test them. How lucky that Artemis and her best friends were in the same class and that they'd all been assigned to this section of the woods!

Defeating three beasts today would mean an A for each of the four girls. Getting only two was a B, one a C, and coming up empty meant having to repeat the test until they got it right. Artemis had never ever got less than an A in the Beast-ology games, and she didn't want this to be an exception. Today was her birthday, after all. Another A would be the perfect gift to herself.

As she entered a clearing, Artemis heard a

snuffling sound. The grey-green leaves of a nearby grove of olive trees rustled, disturbing finches and warblers, which flew away in a great flutter of wings. She slowed, motioning silently to her friends to alert them that something was up.

"It's lurking. Over there!" Artemis called softly as the others drew up beside her. Just then the wind changed direction, and she got a whiff of the creature. *Ugh.* It smelled like pond weed, wet dog and cow pats all rolled into one.

Persephone groaned and fanned her hand in front of her naturally pale face, causing the fringe of her curly red hair to flutter. "Doesn't exactly smell like flowers, does it?" A skilled gardener, she could make anything bloom at the touch of a finger.

Athena wrinkled her nose. "No, it's more like a skunk."

"I hope it doesn't turn out to be something that slings slime this time," whispered Aphrodite. Flipping her long, shiny blonde hair over one shoulder, she touched the gold braid edging the neckline of her chiton. "This outfit is new and I don't want it ruined." The goddessgirl of beauty, she liked to dress well. She had an outfit for every occasion. This one was a bright robin's-egg blue that matched her eyes. Circling her slender waist was a belt made of woven grapevines. Since Aphrodite set most fashion trends at Mount Olympus Academy, every goddessgirl at school would probably be wearing a belt just like it before the end of the week.

*Stomp. Stomp. Stomp.* The ground shook as the beast lumbered closer. Goosebumps rose on Artemis's arms. She'd rather eat a scarab beetle than admit it aloud, but she was scared. Because she was goddess of the hunt and was skilled at archery, everyone at school assumed she was brave. Her friends depended on her to lead them in these hunts. Even now the others were waiting for her to tell them what kind of beast they'd found. And she had a hunch she knew what it was!

Raising her left hand overhead, she held up one finger. Then, after a moment's pause, two fingers. Another pause. Three fingers. And finally, four. Then, holding up her other hand, she showed two more fingers to make six in all. This signalled to the others that they'd probably found a one-headed, two-armed, three-bodied, four-winged, six-legged beast. Just in case they hadn't got the message, she silently mouthed the beast's name: *Geryon*.

At the news, Athena got the determined look on her face that she always had just before taking a test she wanted to ace. Persephone pinched her nose closed, as if preparing for the worst smell ever to get even worse as their opponent came closer. And Aphrodite glanced down at her stylish blue chiton, looking more than a trifle concerned.

Seconds later a giant creature jumped out of the woods into the clearing. At the sight of it, goosebumps rose on top of the goosebumps Artemis already had. The Geryon was big. It was bad. It was beastly. It looked just like the one whose features she'd memorised from her Beast-ology textscroll.

Although she loved to hunt, she wished they'd shoot at normal targets. Sometimes the beasts Professor Ladon designed for these tests seemed so ... so *real*. She struggled to remember that they were fake.

"You called this one right as usual," confirmed

Athena from behind her. "Watch out, the class textscroll says they have particularly vicious talons and wily ways."

"And bad breath," added Aphrodite, holding her nose now along with Persephone.

The Geryon licked its green lips, eyeing them each in turn. Then it turned and waggled its three rear ends so its trio of long tails swept back and forth in the leaves. "Nah nah nuh *nah* nah," it taunted softly. All the while, its blazing red eyes watched them over its shoulder to see if they'd take the bait and move closer. When they didn't, it reached a hand towards them. It poked one foreclaw out and curled it over and over, beckoning them to follow it into the intricate maze of bushes beyond it known as the labyrinth. There was rumoured to be some sort of fantastical beast-making machine in the centre, which Professor Ladon had specially designed to spawn their opponents for these games.

"Ye gods," Athena whispered. "Does it really think we'll fall for that?"

"There's no way we're following it into that maze," Artemis agreed, her voice shaking. Then, worried that her words might have sounded cowardly, she added in a confident voice, "Let's try to lure it closer. I'd like to get a good shot at that big green bottom."

# ABOUT THE AUTHORS

JOAN HOLUB says that of the four Goddess Girls, she's probably most like Athena because she loves to think up new ideas for books. But she's very glad that her dad was never the headmaster at her school!

SUZANNE WILLIAMS asked her husband what she was the goddess of, and he said, "Of asking silly questions!" (Suzanne says they're mostly about why her computer is misbehaving.) That makes her kind of like Pandora, except that Pandora never had to deal with computers. Like Persephone, she also loves flowers, but she doesn't have Persephone's green fingers.